Elizabeth, Larry
and Ed

For Melissa, Kristin, Shannon and Lauren

SIMON & SCHUSTER BOOKS FOR YOUNG READERS
Simon & Schuster Building, Rockefeller Center
1230 Avenue of the Americas, New York, New York 10020
Text copyright © 1992 by Marilyn Sadler
Illustrations copyright © 1992 by Roger Bollen
All rights reserved including the right of reproduction
in whole or in part in any form.
SIMON & SCHUSTER BOOKS FOR YOUNG READERS
is a trademark of Simon & Schuster.
Designed by Vicki Kalajian
The text of this book is set in 16 pt. Clarendon Light.
The illustrations were done in Mixed Media.
Manufactured in the United States of America.

10 9 8 7 6 5 4 3 2 1

Library of Congress Cataloging-in-Publication Data
Sadler, Marilyn. Elizabeth and Larry and Ed / by Marilyn Sadler ;
illustrated by Roger Bollen. p. cm. Summary: An unusual swamp
animal moves in with a human couple when he loses his home
to developers. [1. Swamp animals—Fiction. 2. Wildlife
conservation—Fiction. 3. Florida—Fiction.]
I. Bollen, Roger, ill. II. Title. PZ7.S1239Em
1992 [E]—dc20 91-34142 CIP
ISBN: 0-671-75956-6

Elizabeth, Larry and Ed

By Marilyn Sadler
Illustrated by Roger Bollen

SIMON & SCHUSTER BOOKS FOR YOUNG READERS
Published by Simon & Schuster
New York London Toronto Sydney Tokyo Singapore

Elizabeth and Larry lived in Florida on the edge of a swamp, as well as on the edge of a golf course.

Elizabeth loved the swamp and all of the unusual creatures that lived there. She could spend an entire day just paddling around in a rowboat.

Larry loved the game of golf and all of the unusual people who played it. He could spend an entire day just driving around in a golf cart.

Every evening after dinner, Elizabeth and
Larry talked about the many things they had
experienced that day. Elizabeth always had
something new to show Larry. Larry always
had something new to show Elizabeth.

But as their neighborhood grew larger, Elizabeth's swamp grew smaller and Larry's golf course more crowded. Elizabeth worried about swamp life. Larry worried about tee time.

Then one evening Larry came home for dinner, and Elizabeth had something new to show him.

His name was Ed. He told Elizabeth that he
had lived in the swamp all of his life. But
now he was losing his home to houses like
Elizabeth and Larry's.

Elizabeth was kind enough to invite him to
move in.

From the very start, Larry was not happy
about Ed. Ed was muddy. He was covered with
moss. And he left spots on all of the furniture.

Before the first night was over, Ed had
discovered the television and the refrigerator,
as well as Larry's pajamas and slippers.

And when it was time for bed, Ed insisted on sleeping in Larry's room.

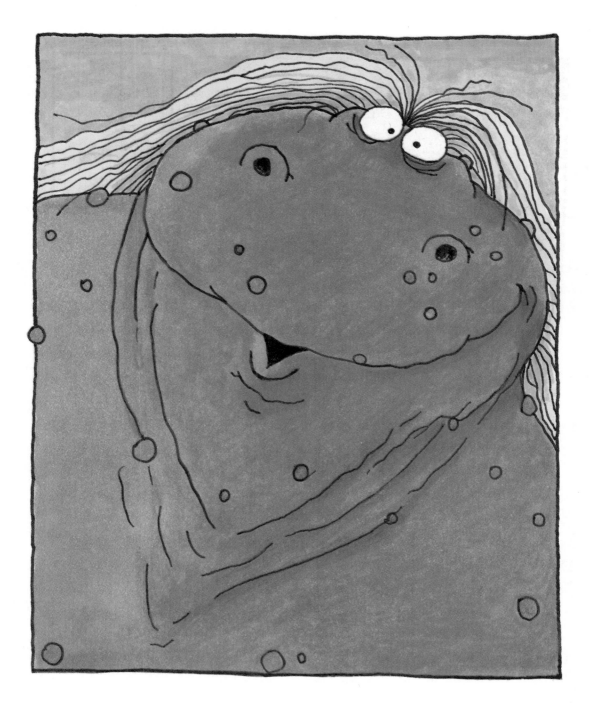

The next morning when Larry opened his
eyes, Ed was the first thing he saw.

The second thing he saw was the mess Ed made in the bathroom.

Larry was so upset, he had his toast and
orange juice at the club.

Larry's day didn't get much better either. All of the golf carts were taken. He missed a one inch-putt. And an alligator ate his golf ball.

When Larry came home that evening, he was disappointed to find that Ed was still there. He was also disappointed to find that Ed had borrowed his swimsuit.

That night all Ed could talk about was his life back in the swamp. All Larry could think about was Ed back in the swamp.

The next morning, just when Larry
thought things couldn't get much worse,
Ed discovered the game of golf.

Larry had no choice but to take Ed with him to the golf course that day. This meant that Ed needed a hat. Ed needed the shoes with the spikes. Ed needed his own set of golf clubs.

Ed insisted on driving the golf cart.

And when Ed finally hit his first golf ball,
his club went with it.

At first Elizabeth thought that Ed would
be a nice friend for Larry. But now she could
see that she had been wrong.

Elizabeth did not know what to do. Ed was
a wonderful creature. But she could not bear
to see Larry so unhappy.

Then, to Elizabeth's surprise, Ed's mother appeared at the door. It seemed that Ed had forgotten to mention her.

Ed's mother was very angry with her son. He had not told Elizabeth the whole truth. Though they were losing their home, they were moving to a new home in a part of the swamp that had been set aside for swamp creatures just like them.

Elizabeth was happy to know that not only did Ed have a home, but he had a very nice mother as well.

Larry could not have been happier. He helped
Ed pack all of his things. He even let Ed keep
his pajamas.

Elizabeth and Larry hugged Ed good-bye. Although Larry was happy to see Ed go, he thought there was a slight chance he might miss him.

That afternoon Larry played his best
game of golf ever. He even made his first
hole in one.

Elizabeth was happy, too. After all, Larry
was himself again. Ed was home with his
mother. And there was a special place set
aside in the swamp...

...for all of its unusual creatures.